Copyright © 2004 by Michael Neugebauer Verlag,
an imprint of Nord-Süd Verlag AG, Gossau Zürich, Switzerland
First published in Switzerland under the title *Papa, was ist das?*
English translation copyright © 2005 by North-South Books Inc.
All rights reserved. No part of this book may be reproduced or utilized in
any form or by any means, electronic or mechanical, including photocopying,
recording, or any information storage and retrieval system, without
permission in writing from the publisher.
First published in the United States, Great Britain, Canada,
Australia, and New Zealand in 2005 by North-South Books,
an imprint of Nord-Süd Verlag AG, Gossau Zürich, Switzerland.
Distributed in the United States by North-South Books Inc., New York.
Library of Congress Cataloging-in-Publication Data is available.
A CIP catalogue record for this book is available from The British Library.
ISBN 0-7358-1980-7 (trade edition) 10 9 8 7 6 5 4 3 2 1
ISBN 0-7358-1981-5 (library edition) 10 9 8 7 6 5 4 3 2 1
Printed in Belgium
For more information about our books, and the authors and artists
who create them, visit our web site: www.northsouth.com

Wiggles

By Christophe Loupy
Illustrated by Eve Tharlet

NORTH-SOUTH BOOKS / NEW YORK / LONDON

Cock-a-doodle-doo!
As soon as the rooster crowed one morning,
Father quietly got up. Wiggles was wide awake, too.
"Where are you going?" she asked.
"Shhh!" whispered Father. "Don't wake the others.
I'm going for a walk. Come with me."

In the yard, the farmer's wife
was already at work.
"Where is she going?" asked Wiggles.
"Wait and see, Wiggles," Father replied.

In the barn, the farmer's wife
began to milk the cow.
"What is she doing?" asked
Wiggles.
"Wait!" said Father.
But Wiggles was too curious to wait.
She moved closer, and a few drops
of milk landed on her tongue.
"Yumm! That's good!" said Wiggles.

Suddenly, there was a loud buzzing noise outside.
"What is *that*?" asked Wiggles.
"Let's go outside and see," said Father.
But Wiggles saw a quicker way. She scampered
up the coal pile and looked out of the window.
A red helicopter flew right over the farm, making
a terrible racket.

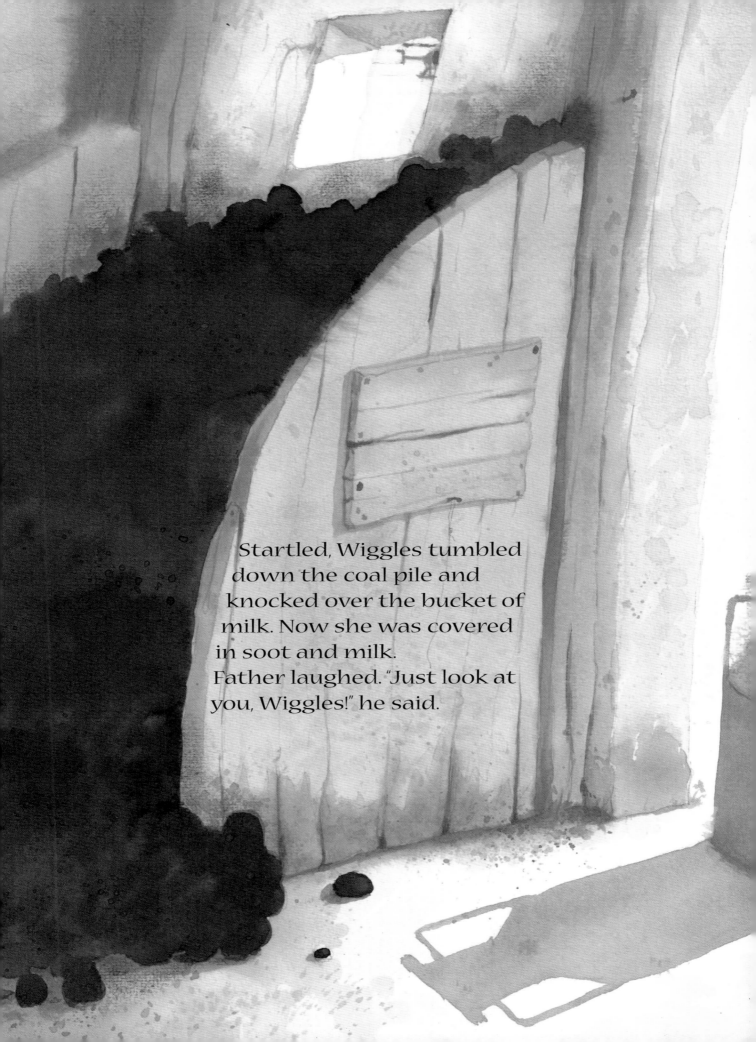

Startled, Wiggles tumbled
down the coal pile and
knocked over the bucket of
milk. Now she was covered
in soot and milk.
Father laughed. "Just look at
you, Wiggles!" he said.

Wiggles and Father headed out to the farmyard.
They saw the farmer's wife carrying a basket.
"Where is she going now?" asked Wiggles.
"Wait and see," Father replied.
Wiggles followed, wiggling with excitement.

When they reached the chicken coop, Wiggles watched
the farmer's wife collect eggs.
Wiggles went to investigate. She pushed her nose right
into a nest.
"Watch out!" warned Father.
Too late! Wiggles fell into the nest, breaking the eggs.

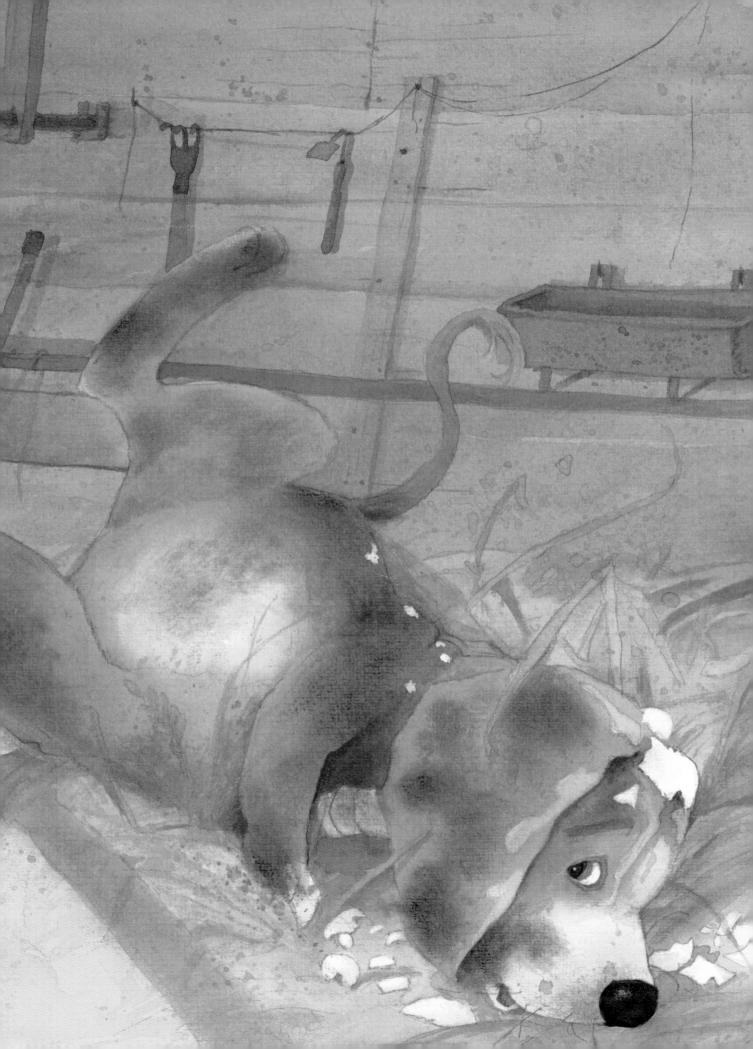

"Eggs are good, too!" said Wiggles, happily
licking the egg off her face.
Father gave her a lick.
"Yes, they're delicious!" he said. "And so are you!"
Just then, the farmer's wife headed out to
the orchard.
"Where is she going?" asked Wiggles.
"Let's see," Father replied.

They followed the farmer's wife to the orchard.
"Those houses are pretty!" exclaimed Wiggles.
"Don't go near them!" warned Father. "They're
beehives, and bees don't like to be disturbed."
"I'm just going to say hello," said Wiggles.

Wiggles poked her nose into one of the hives. When she pulled it back out, it was covered with honey. "Mmm! That smells good!" said Wiggles.

The bees buzzed angrily all around her. "Help!" cried Wiggles, and ran away as fast as she could.

Wiggles raced to the pond. She bent down to take a drink. "Oh!" she exclaimed. "Who is that?"
"Don't you recognize her?" asked Father.
"No. She's black, white, and yellow and wearing a funny hat!"
Wiggles bent over to look closer and . . . *plop!* tumbled into the pond.

"Ha!" exclaimed Father. "Well, you really needed a bath."

"Look! I can swim!" Wiggles said proudly. Father jumped in, too. Then he and Wiggles played hide-and-seek among the water lilies.

When they got back to the farm,
Mother and the other puppies
were just waking up. Wiggles
snuggled against her mother.
"I had milk and eggs and honey
and I went swimming, too,"
she told her.

"What a nice dream you had!" said Mother,
giving Wiggles a soft kiss. "But what are you
going to do now that it's time to get up?"
"Wait and see . . ." said Wiggles, yawning.
And she fell fast asleep.